For Kaarel

First American Edition 2017
Kane Miller, A Division of EDC Publishing

Shh! My Brother's Napping. Copyright © 2014 by Ruth Ohi.
All rights reserved.
Published by arrangement with Scholastic Canada Limited.

For information contact:
Kane Miller, A Division of EDC Publishing
PO Box 470663
Tulsa, OK 74147-0663
www.kanemiller.com
www.edcpub.com
www.usbornebooksandmore.com

Library of Congress Control Number: 2016934253

Printed in China
1 2 3 4 5 6 7 8 9 10

ISBN: 978-1-61067-552-9

Shh! My Brother's Napping

Ruth Ohi

Kane Miller
A DIVISION OF EDC PUBLISHING

Shh! My brother's napping.
He really needs his sleep.
He was grumbly as a grouch,
and now lies in a heap.

He's very noisy when he sleeps.
His mouth hangs open wide.
But Mommy has forbidden me
from putting things inside.

Shh! Your brother's napping.

We must be very thoughtful,
and do our very best
to keep the house a quiet place
and let my brother rest.

Shh! Your brother's napping.

Reading stories can be quiet.
Reading's calm and makes me dream.

Unless there's a scary part
that makes me run and —

Shh! Your brother's napping.

Painting pictures can be quiet.
Color brightly filling space.

But Mommy says to keep the art
off brother's sleeping face.

Shh! Your brother's napping.

So I will just play quietly,
and build my little town.

The blocks and books will sit so still.
Unless they all . . .

Ooops!

I didn't mean to wake him.
I'm sorry for the noise.
But now that brother's wide-awake,
let's bring out all the toys.

Shh! My brother's napping.